TROUBLEMAKER

Dianne Bates

Illustrated by Marina McAllan

A Haights Cross Communications Company

For information regarding permission, write to:
Sundance Publishing
P.O. Box 740
One Beeman Road
Northborough, MA 01532

Published by:
Sundance Publishing
P.O. Box 740
One Beeman Road
Northborough, MA 01532

First published 1996 by
Addison Wesley Longman Australia Pty Limited
95 Coventry Street
South Melbourne 3205 Australia
Exclusive United States Distribution: Sundance Publishing

ISBN 0-7608-0768-X

CONTENTS

for Sarah Viney

CHAPTER 1

DUMBO

There's this girl at my school, and everyone hates her. She's always in trouble. Her name's Katy Hassell, but she gets called "Dumbo" or "Satellite Dish" because of her stick-out cars.

One day Katy Hassell nearly got expelled. It happened like this. Our PE teacher, Mr. Amour, had us jumping over the vaulting box. I was first in line.

"Well done, Anna Roonie," Mr. Amour said as I cleared the box by about ten inches.

Everyone cheered.

Katy wouldn't even try. Mr. Amour kept at her, and at her, to try.

"Katy Hassell, don't just stand there!" he said.

Katy wouldn't move. So Mr. Amour yelled at her.

Katy told him to grow a brain. She also said some other things I can't repeat.

Boy, was she in BIG TROUBLE!

Sometimes Katy says cruel things to the kids in our class. Like the time Dean Mitakos told her she looked like a VW with the doors open.

Katy replied, "Why don't you tuck your tummy in, fatso?"

Dean is really overweight, but everyone likes him. His face crumpled when she said that.

We all felt sorry for him.

When my best friend, Crystal, had a birthday party, she invited everyone in our class. But not Katy Hassell.

Katy said she didn't care. After that, she always called Crystal "Jelly Crystal."

When the teacher isn't looking, Katy sticks her tongue out at her.

In social studies, she makes jokes about
Abraham Lincoln like calling him a warty hairy
broomstick. Alexandra told on her last week.

"You're a troublemaker, Katy Hassell,"
Mrs. Giles said. She tried to make Katy
apologize to the social studies teacher. But
Katy refused. She closed her mouth tightly
and wouldn't say a word.

Mrs. Giles said, "Right, Miss, you're on detention for two weeks. Maybe this will teach you a lesson."

Katy mumbled something under her breath on her way back to her seat.

Laura Tosi, Sonia Bianco, and Tammy Belmont told on her. Mrs. Giles said she was sending for Katy's mother. But Mrs. Hassell never came, even after Mrs. Giles sent a letter home.

ON DETENTION

One day, when Katy was on detention, I was sent to stand in the corridor, too. It was the first time in my life I'd ever been in real trouble at school.

"How come you're on detention, Miss Goody Two-Shoes?" Katy said.

I told her it was a big mistake. Jason Pendergast kept calling me "Stupid." He bugs me all the time just because I'm not a very good reader. Every time I stumble on a word, he mumbles, "Stupid." It drives me crazy, so I hit him.

"Good one!" Katy said. "I would have whacked him too, big smarty-pants."

While we were standing in the corridor, Jason came over and teased both of us.

"Dumbo and Stupid, what a mega-combination!" he said.

"Get lost, rat-face," Katy replied.

I pushed Jason. The air whooshed out of him.
He fell backwards and hit his head on the wall.

Some younger kids saw. They ran outside
screaming, "Anna Roonie pushed Jason
Pendergast. And he hit his head really hard.
He's dead!"

I didn't mean for Jason to hit his head. I tried to tell Mrs. Giles, but she wouldn't listen.

"You're on detention for two weeks, Anna Roonie!" she said. "I can't think what's gotten into you, today."

CHAPTER 3

EVERYONE PICKS ON ME

Katy said she was pleased I would keep her company on detention. But my best friend, Crystal, was not impressed.

"I don't like bullies," she said. "Emily's my best friend from now on."

I tried to explain to her what happened. But she walked away.

Crystal and I had been friends since first grade.
My throat felt like it was full of razor blades.
A lump as big as a fist formed in my stomach.

It was not fair! Nobody felt sorry for me.
Except Katy.

"You're not stupid," Katy said. "Jason
Pendergast got what he deserved."

After lunch I tried to talk to Crystal. She wouldn't talk to me. No one would. Except Katy.

I loaned her my sketch pads, and she drew a funny picture. It was a dragon with fire spurting from its mouth. Underneath it she wrote, MRS. GILES IN A BAD MOOD.

I'd never noticed before, but Katy's a really good drawer.

Mrs. Giles saw Katy drawing. "Bring that to me, Katy Hassell," she said.

Mrs. Giles was not impressed at being drawn like a fiery dragon.

She made Katy write out "I must improve my manners" two hundred times.

The rest of the class went out to play softball. "I don't care," Katy said. "I didn't want to play softball, anyway."

Spiros and Lenka were the captains.
Neither of them wanted me on their team.

"Not after what she did to Jason," Spiros said.
Lenka said she didn't want any friend of Katy
Hassell's on her team.

I felt really hurt. Usually I'm one of the first
picked. I told Lenka I wouldn't be on her team,
even if she paid me a million dollars.

But Mrs. Giles told me to stop sulking and to go and stand in the outfield.

I stood there. But whenever a ball came near me, I refused to touch it. Everyone on Lenka's team yelled at me. But I pretended I didn't care.

CHAPTER 4

IN TROUBLE AGAIN

The next day no one wanted to play with me.
They said things like, "Why don't you play with
your friend, Katy Hassell?"
I said, "Why don't you drop dead?"
"You sound just like Katy," Crystal said.

People kept picking on me all day. They told lies about me. Marcus Nightingale said I stuck my foot out on purpose to trip him up. Sky Marshall told everyone I hit Jason Pendergast with a rock. And *she* wasn't even at school when the accident happened.

The *worst* thing was when Kim Fong said
I smelled. Everyone started chanting,
"Anna Roonie smells!"

I felt so hurt I wanted to run home. None of the teachers would listen to me. I was fed up with everyone. Katy Hassell was my only friend.

At lunchtime, on the way to detention, Katy and I played Vampires. We imagined we were in charge of the world. Everyone had to do what we said. And if they didn't, we would get them in the middle of the night.

Mary Russ told Mr. Symes we were tormenting the younger kids. We were in trouble again!

I tried to explain to the principal it was only a game, but he wouldn't listen. Instead, he lectured me about good manners. He also gave me a letter for my parents.

CHAPTER 5

AT KATY'S HOUSE

I knew the letter was bad news. I wasn't in a hurry to deliver it, so I asked Katy if I could go over to her house after school.

Katy said she had to look after her five younger brothers and sisters.

I like little kids. I said I'd help.

Katy sounded exasperated. "I have to make dinner, too, you know," she said.

I told her that was okay. "I never get to make meals at my place. It sounds like fun," I said.

"My mother's sick," Katy said. "It might be catching."

I didn't care. Anything would be better than the hour-long lecture I knew Mom and Dad would give me when they read Mr. Symes' letter.

"I *really* want to come over. Today!" I said.

"Oh, okay then," Katy replied.

She didn't sound very keen on it though.

I'd never been to Katy's before. We had to walk a long way.

I asked Katy why she didn't catch a bus to school. Katy didn't answer. But I'm sure she heard me. She was in a funny mood. Very quiet. Not like her usual, noisy self.

My house is two-story brick. The yard is pretty with trees, flowers, and a trimmed lawn.

Katy's house was old and falling down. Her front yard was filled with knee-high weeds and junk like rusty toys, tin cans, and soggy newspapers.

Inside the house, Mrs. Hassell was yelling. She was really squawking. I bet you could hear her way down the street. Boy, did she have a temper!

Katy's twin brothers were climbing a tree.

"Get down from there, you rotten kids," Mrs. Hassell screamed.

"Wayne, if you do that again, so help me I'll give you a spanking," screamed Mrs. Hassell.

I wished I hadn't invited myself to Katy's. I wished I'd gone straight home.

Katy looked sideways at me. I'm sure she was embarrassed. She probably thought I'd tell everyone about her shabby house and her screaming mother.

We went inside. Mrs. Hassell was still yelling at Wayne. Two whining kids clung to her dress.

When I bring a friend home, my Mom always makes a fuss of them. But Mrs. Hassell ignored me.

She snapped at Katy about taking so long to get home.

I couldn't wait to get out of there.

CHAPTER 6

MOM AND DAD HELP

That night Mom and Dad talked to me about Mr. Symes' letter. I promised them my behavior would improve.

"Mr. Symes says you're usually well-behaved," Dad said. "Perhaps Katy Hassell is encouraging you to be naughty."

I told Mom and Dad about Katy. How she lived in an ugly house. How her mother screamed all the time, even when she had visitors. How Katy had all these brothers and sisters. How she almost always had to look after them. How everyone at school picked on her.

Mom said it sounded as though Katy was a very unhappy little girl.

"You can invite her here anytime you like," she said.

I snuggled into Mom. "I'm glad we have a happy home," I said.

Mom cuddled and kissed me. So did Dad.

That night, for the first time in a long time, they tucked me into bed.

"Sweet dreams, Princess," they said.

I lay awake for a long time thinking about Katy Hassell. Fancy having so many problems, I thought. No wonder Katy gets cranky with people.

I was glad I was Anna Roonie and not Katy Hassell.

CHAPTER 7

FRIENDS AGAIN

The next day at school, I tried talking to Crystal.

"Are you still friends with Katy Hassell?" she said.

I really wanted to be friends with Crystal again. And I didn't want to fight with her about Katy. So I just shrugged my shoulders.

"Emily's not at school today," she said. "You
can play with me, if you like."

I didn't know what to say. The hard little lump
of anger I felt when Crystal ignored me the day
before was still lodged in my chest.

Just then, Katy walked into the schoolyard.
I looked at Katy and I looked at Crystal.
I wanted to be friends with both of them. Who
should I choose?

Across the yard, Katy was acting strangely.
She didn't rush up to me like she had yesterday
and the day before. Instead, she slunk over to the
seats. She sat there, pretending to read a book.
But she kept sneaking quick looks at Crystal and
me.

"Well?" Crystal said. "Do you want to play with me or not?"

I wanted to tell Crystal about Katy and her sad home, her noisy, demanding brothers and sisters, and her monster of a mother who made her work like a slave. But if I did, she'd probably tell everyone else. And they'd have more reasons to pick on Katy.

"I'd like to play with you," I said.

Crystal reached over and took my hand and swung it in an arc. She smiled at me and the knot vanished. It was replaced by a warm glow.

Out of the corner of my eye, I saw Katy staring at us. Her face looked sad, as though she had just lost something precious.

I thought how Katy had been the only person to talk to me when I was in trouble. I couldn't let her down now.

I let go of Crystal's hand. "I'm sorry, Crystal. But if we're going to be friends again, then you have to be friends with Katy, too."

Crystal could see I meant it.

"But she's a troublemaker, Anna," she said.

"Please," I said, "just try to like her. She's really nice when you get to know her."

You could tell Crystal didn't really believe me.

"She calls me 'Jelly Crystal,'" she said.

"But what if I tell her not to?"

Crystal still looked unsure. But after a while, she said, "Oh, okay then. But if she's a pain, I won't play with her. Okay?"

My heart tumbled with happiness. I ran across the playground to Katy.

"Hi Katy!" I called. "Do you want to play with Crystal and me?"

Katy didn't look too sure.

"She didn't invite me to her party," she said, "and she calls me names."

"But you call her 'Jelly Crystal,' and it hurts her feelings."

Katy sat for a long time. She looked at the ground.

"I want to be friends with both of you," I said. "What if I tell her not to call you names. And you agree not to call her 'Jelly Crystal'?"

"Okay then," she agreed.

We ran across the playground. I got Katy and
Crystal to promise not to call each other names.

Then we scrambled up the jungle gym. There we stayed, chattering like three happy magpies. After a while, it was like we'd been friends all our lives.

Crystal didn't call Katy, "Dumbo" or "Satellite Dish" ever again. And Katy never teased Crystal one little bit.

Dianne Bates

Dianne Bates has written more than 40 books for children. As a child she was always in trouble for having her nose stuck in books (mostly those written by Enid Blyton) because she should have been working on her family's poultry farm.

As well as being an author, Di has worked at many other jobs. She has been a social worker in a home for delinquent girls, a factory worker, a bookseller, a teacher, an advertising sales' representative, a journalist, a TV and radio presenter, a dishwasher, and a nurse's assistant.

Di works in schools as a performer, but she also enjoys volunteer work as a welfare counselor.